LEVEL 1 READER

Moo Dog

David Milgrim

SCHOLASTIC INC.

For Joyce.

ISBN 978-0-545-82503-0
10 9 8 7 6 5 4 3 2 16 17 18 19 20

Printed in the U.S.A. 40

First edition, September 2016

Mooooooooooo!

Moooooooooooooo!

Huh?

What are you doing?

Mooing.

But you are not cows.

We know.

Moooooooooooooooo!

Moo!
I hear a cow.
I know.

Moo!
That is not a cow.
I know.

Moo!
Then why is he—
I do not know.

Mooooooooooooooo!
What is going on?
No one knows.

Can I see?
?

Moooooooooooo!
That is not a cow.

It is a dog.
No! It's a **Moo Dog**!

Ha! A Moo Dog!
Tee hee!
?

Hee haw!
Ha, ha!

Ha
Hee
Ho
Ho
Ha
Ha
Ho
Hee
What is so funny?
Ha
Yuk
LOL
Hee

Tee
Ho
Haw
Hee
Ho
Har
Hee
Haw
Yuk

You are funny!
Dogs do not moo!
Yeah, dogs do not moo!

Sure they do.
Huh?
Say what?

Look.

Moooooooooooo!

See?
But—
Um—
Uh—

I am a dog.
And I moo.
You got it?

Yeah—
But—
Um—

My friend said— You got it?

Yeah, okay.

We got it.
You moo.
You both moo.

Mooooooooo!

Mooooooooo!

Moooooooooo!
Cock-a-doodle-doo!